Dedicated to my
little Lion

WIGGAWOOS

Copyright © Wiggawoos book Ltd

All rights reserved. No part of this publication may be reproduced, distributed, or transmitted in any form or by any means, including photocopying or other electronic or mechanical methods, without the prior written permission of the publisher, except in the case of brief quotations embodied in critical reviews and certain other noncommercial uses permitted by copyright law. For permission requests, write to the publisher, wiggawoos@gmail.com

THE LION WHO FOUND HIS ROAR

WRITTEN BY NATHANIEL L BERTRAM

ILLUSTRATED BY SARAH GRACE

There was a lion called Javiah,

Who lived in the jungle.

He had a mum and dad

who loved him more than words could

mumble.

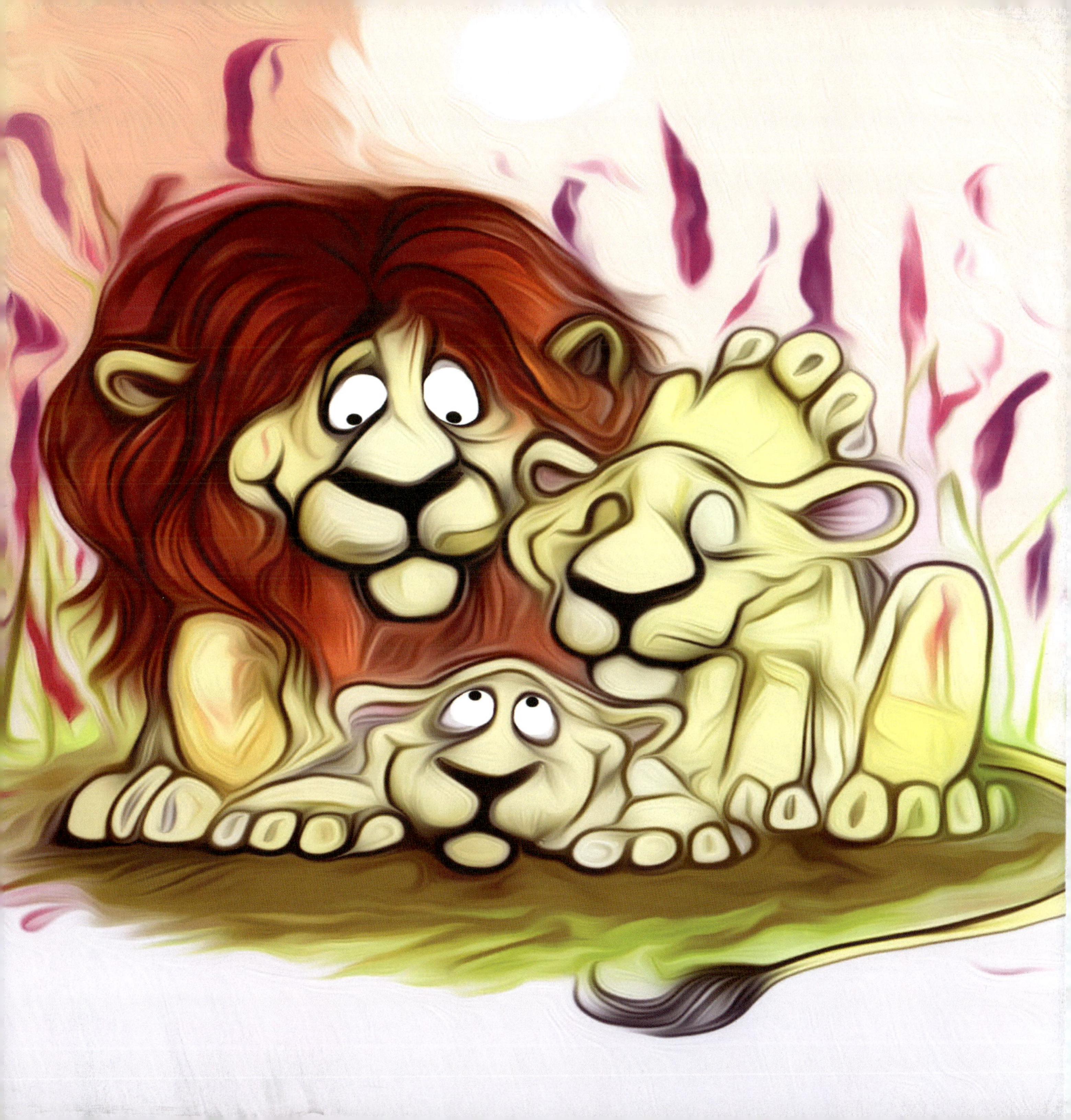

He was polite and grateful,
happy and playful.
But there was one thing about this lion
that was a little but shameful.

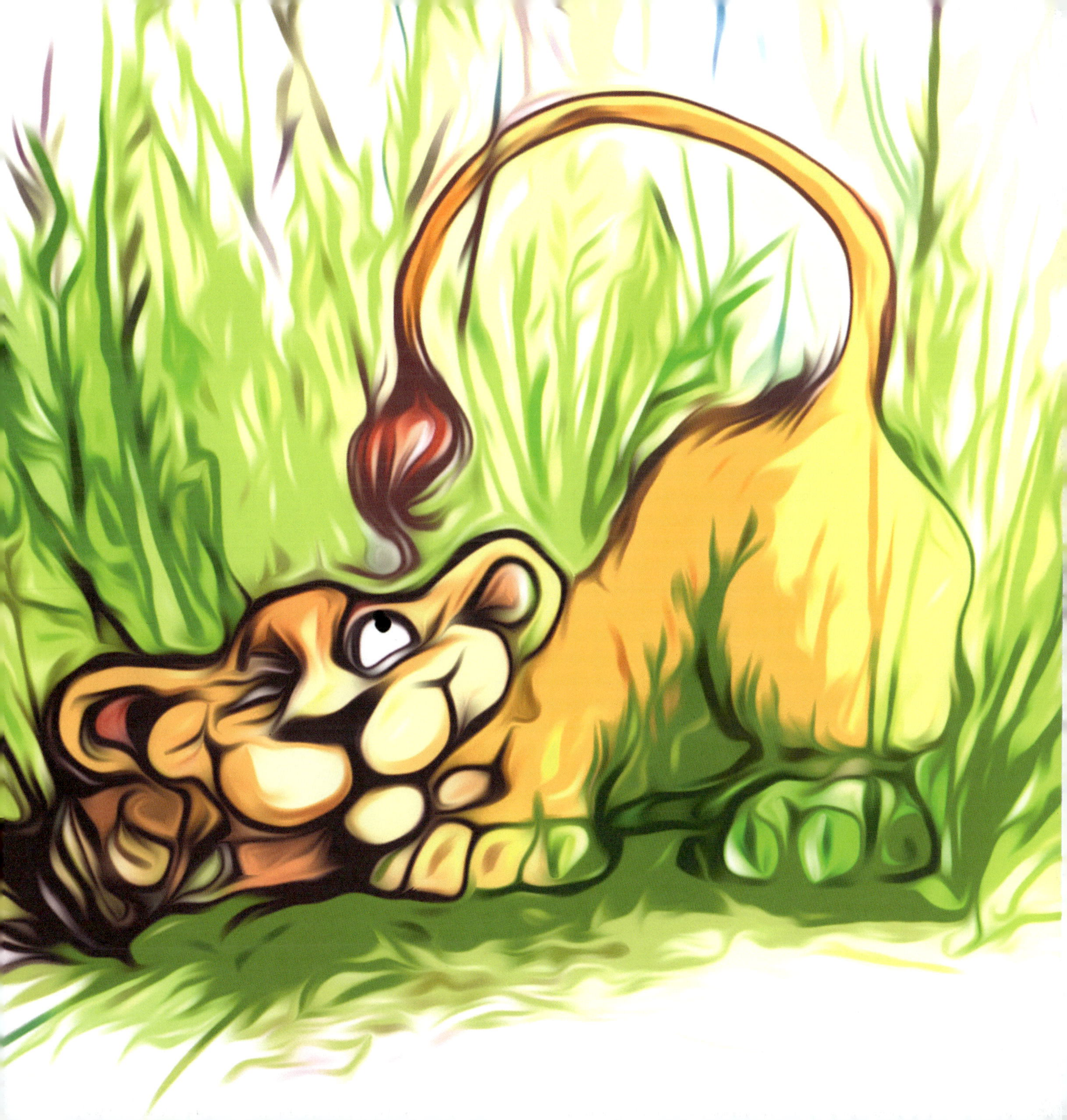

His Dad could roar
for the whole jungle to listen.
But when javiah tried to roar there was
always something missing.

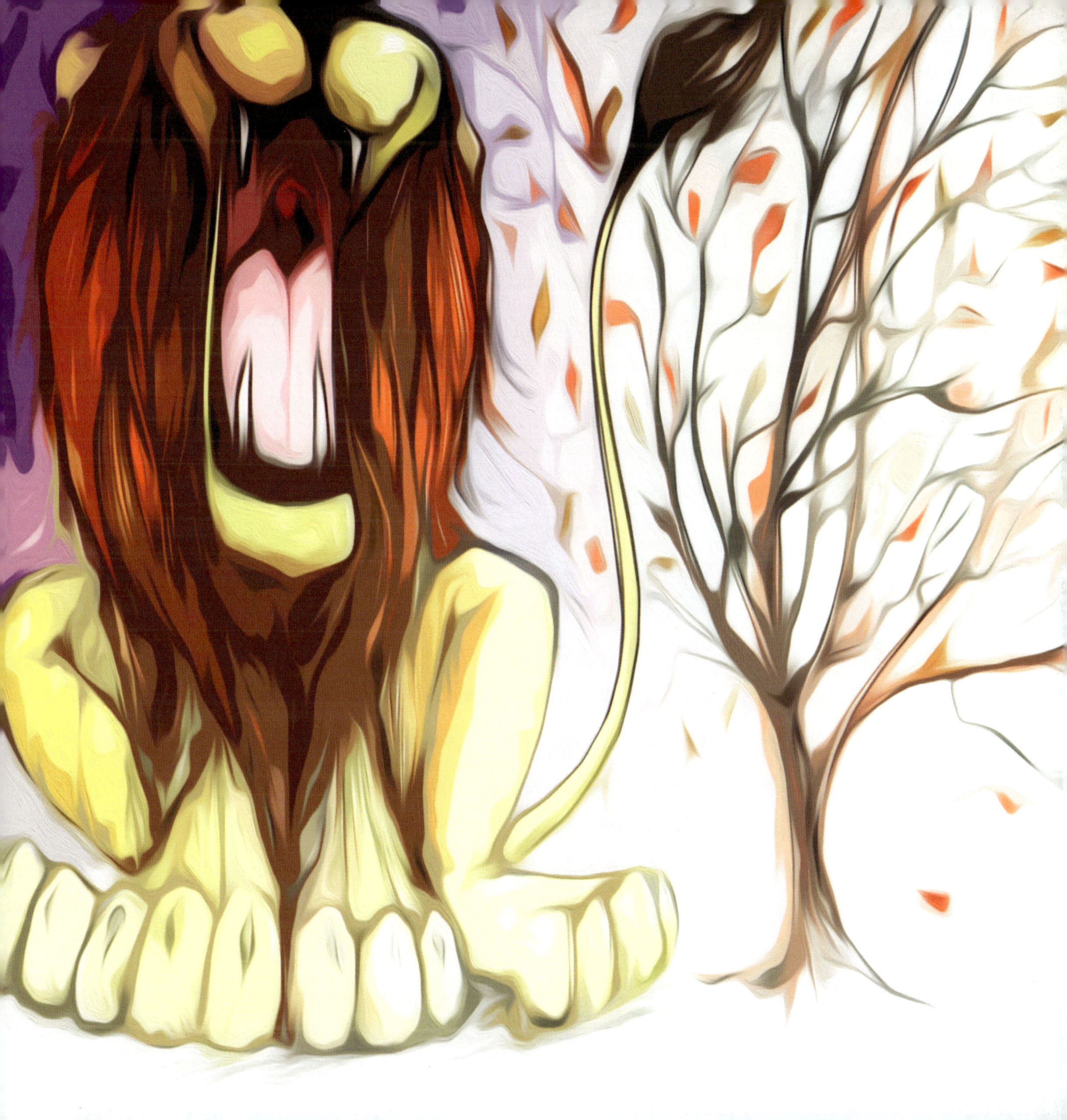

He huffed and he puffed more and more,
But no matter how much he tried
he could not roar.

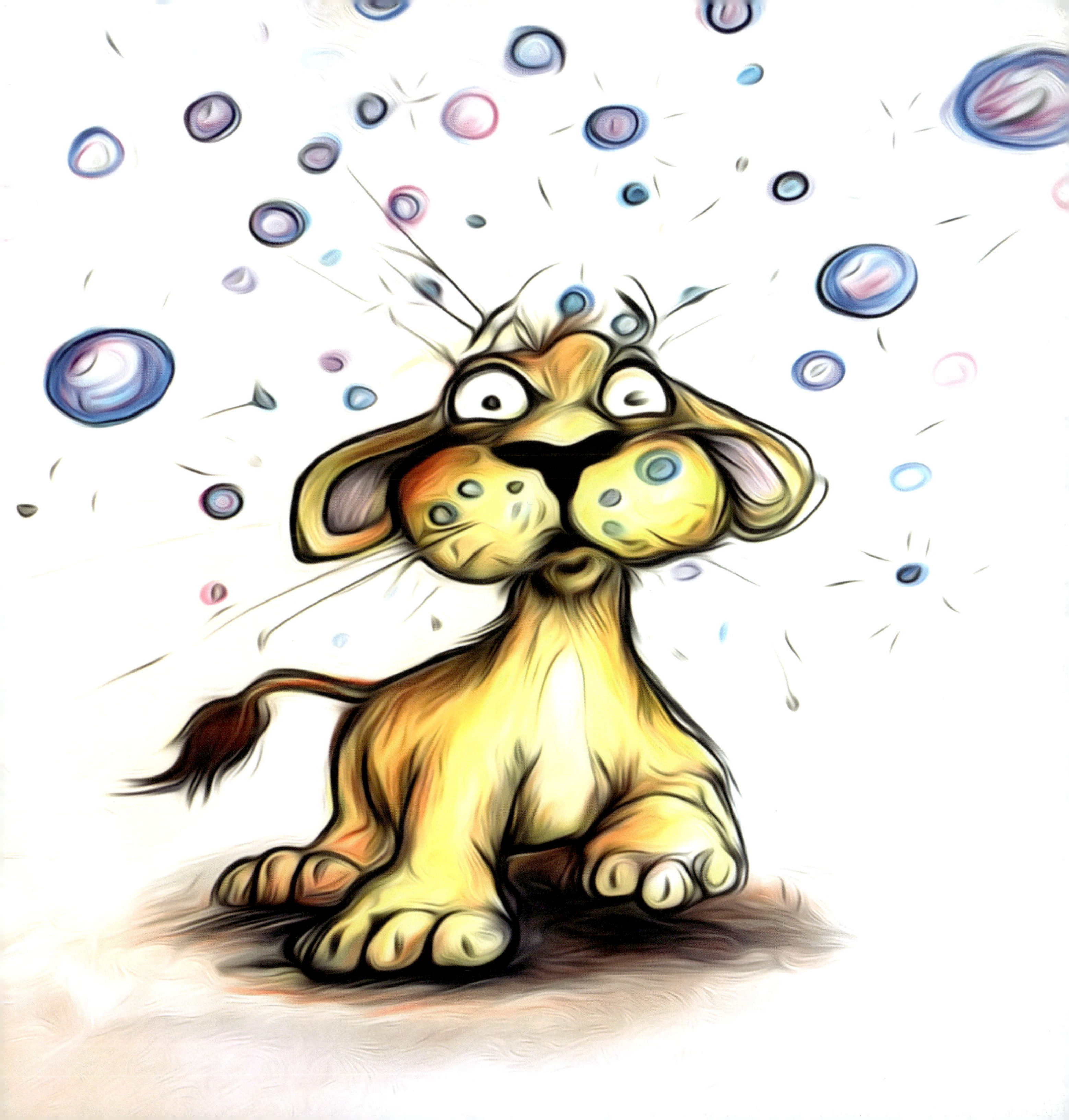

He walked through the jungle
and saw Jaylon the monkey,
Who loved dancing to music
and being funky.

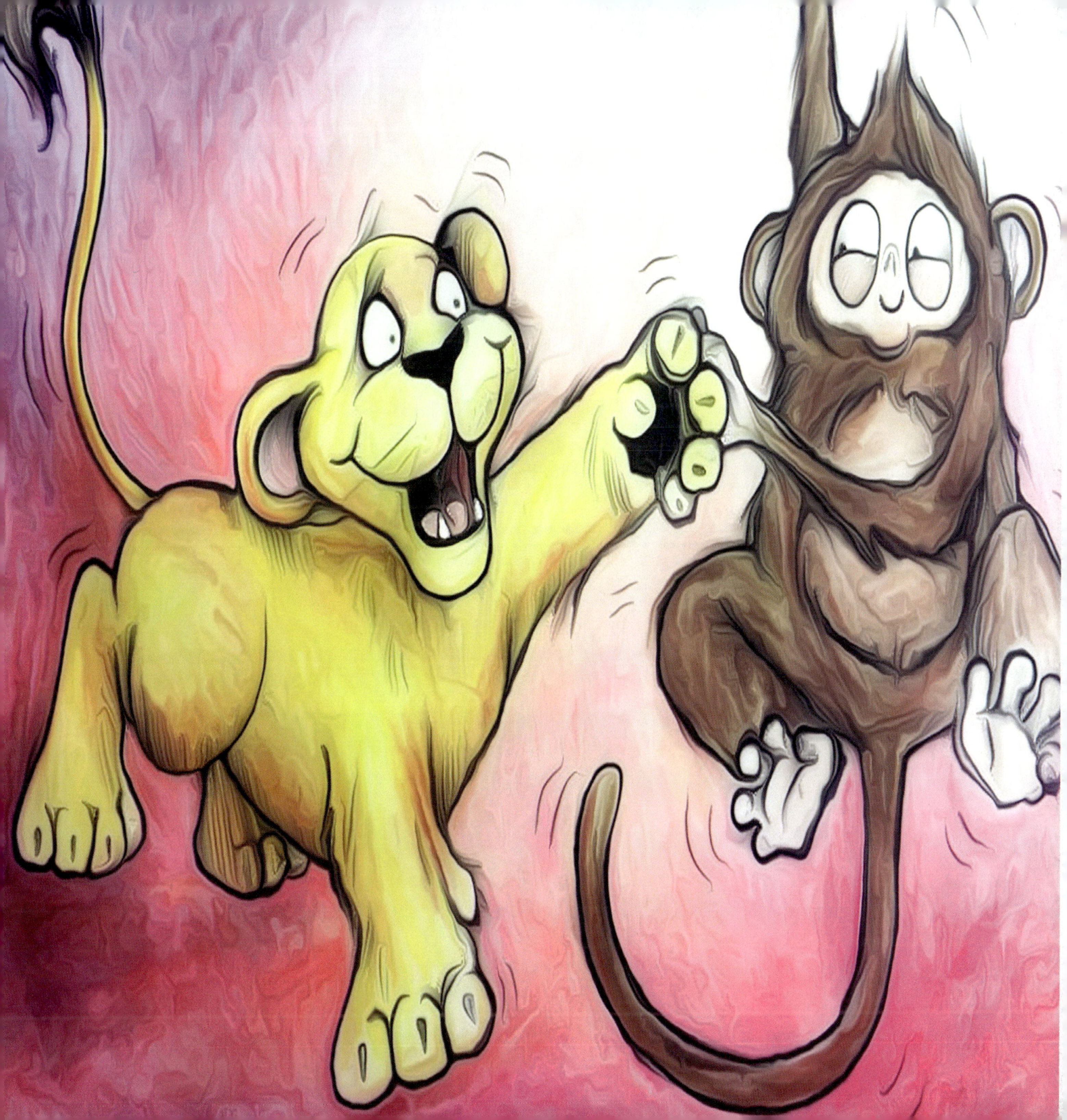

"Can you teach me to roar?"
Javiah then asked.
The monkey replied, "No, but I can teach you to dance!
1 step, 2 step, 3 step, 4.
Left leg, right leg, lift up your paws!"

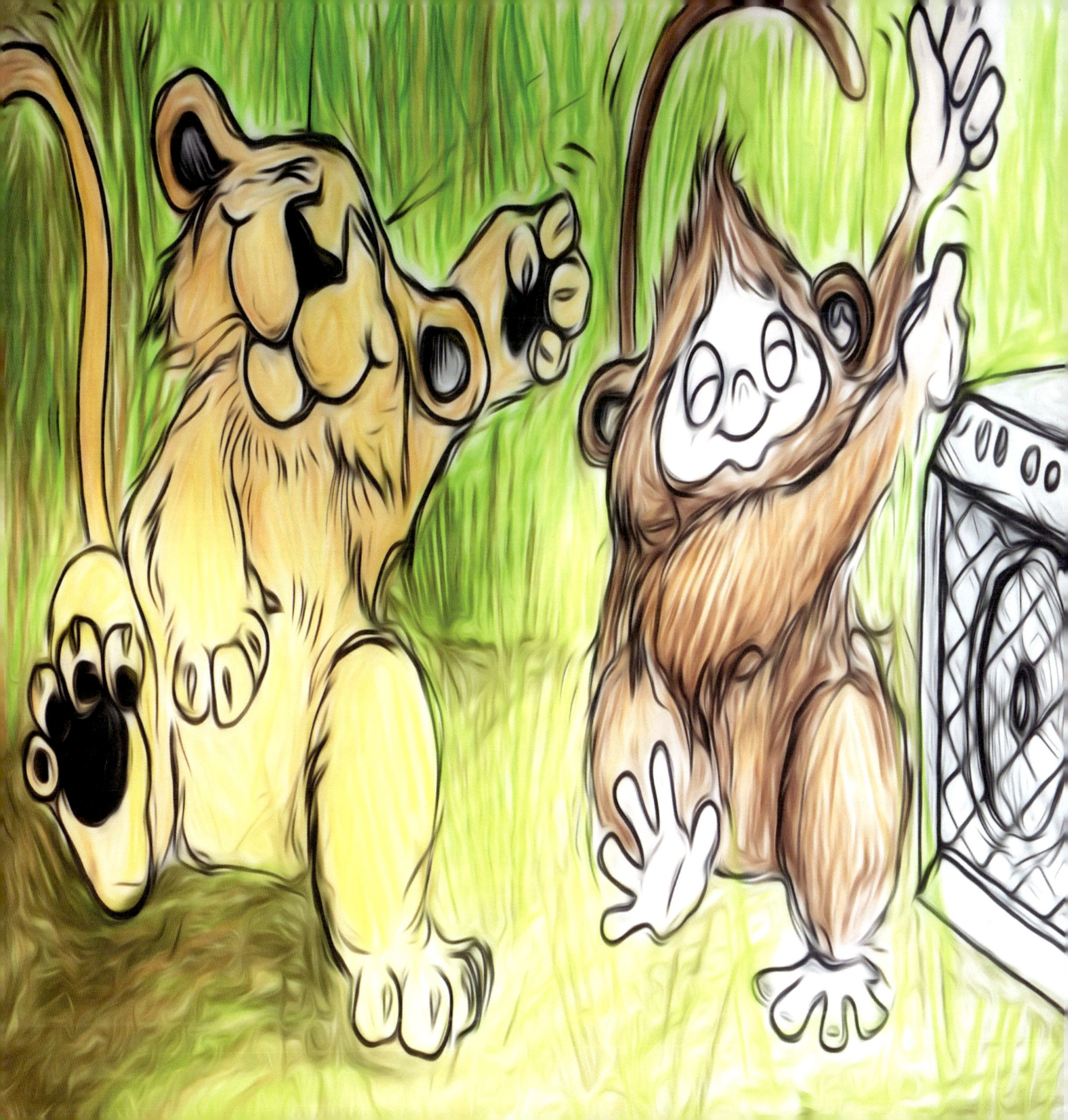

"I like this!" Javiah said,
as he danced on his feet.
Dancing through the jungle
for the next animal to meet.

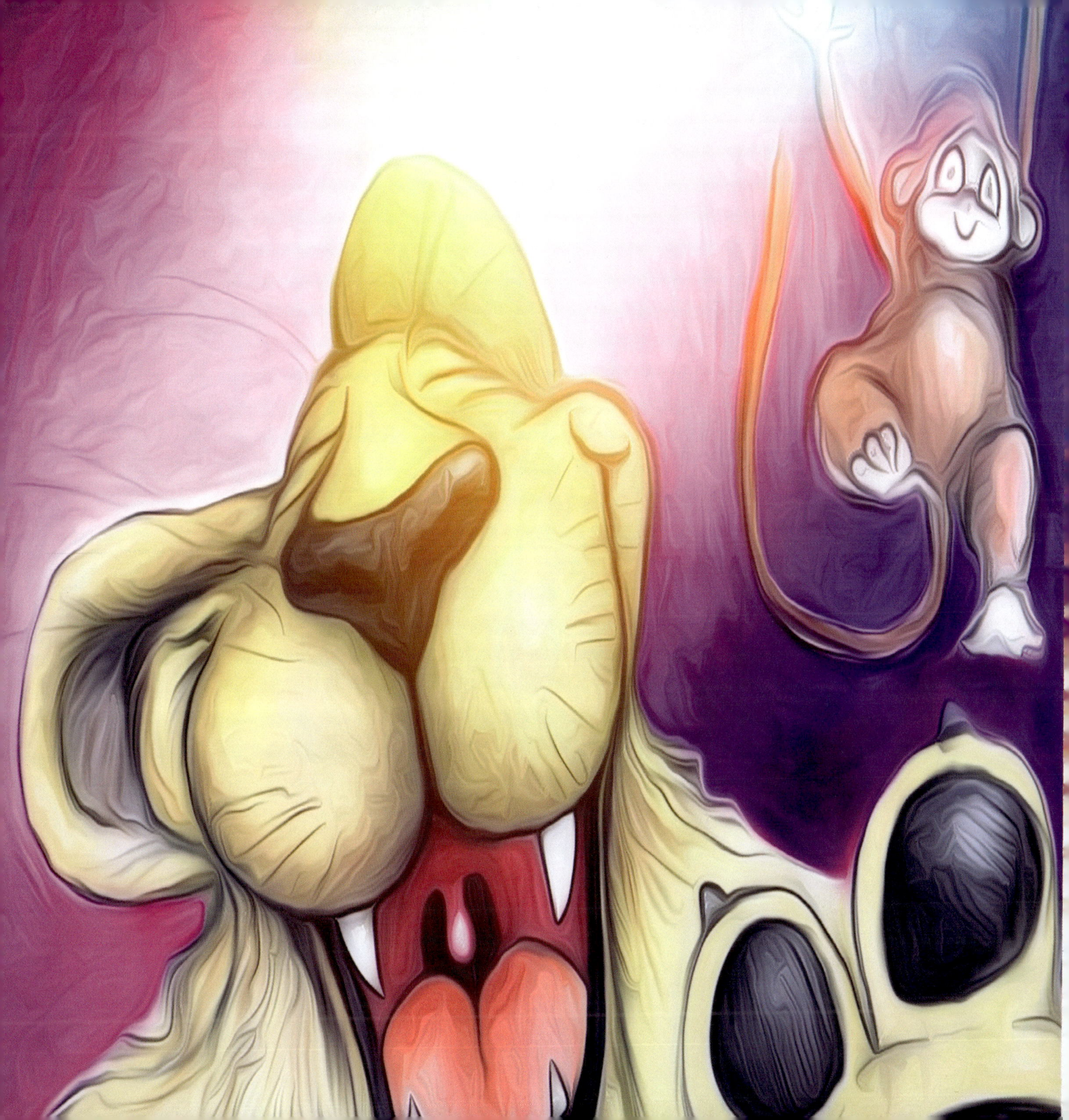

He came across Shacky the elephant, who loved drawing and painting.

He drew a picture of Javiah dancing and it was amazing!

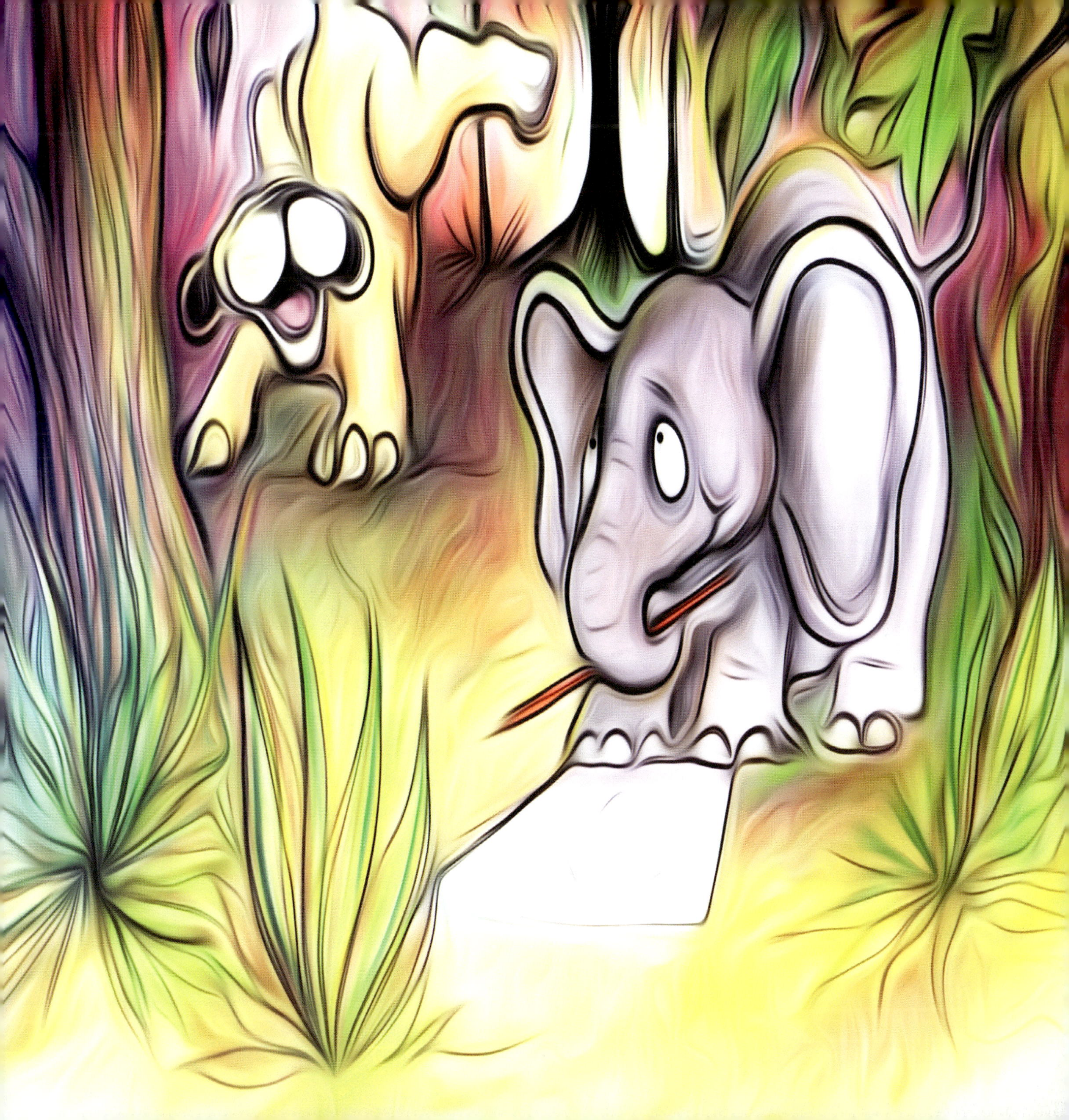

Javiah asked, "Can you teach me to roar?"
The elephant replied,
"No, but I can teach you to draw!"

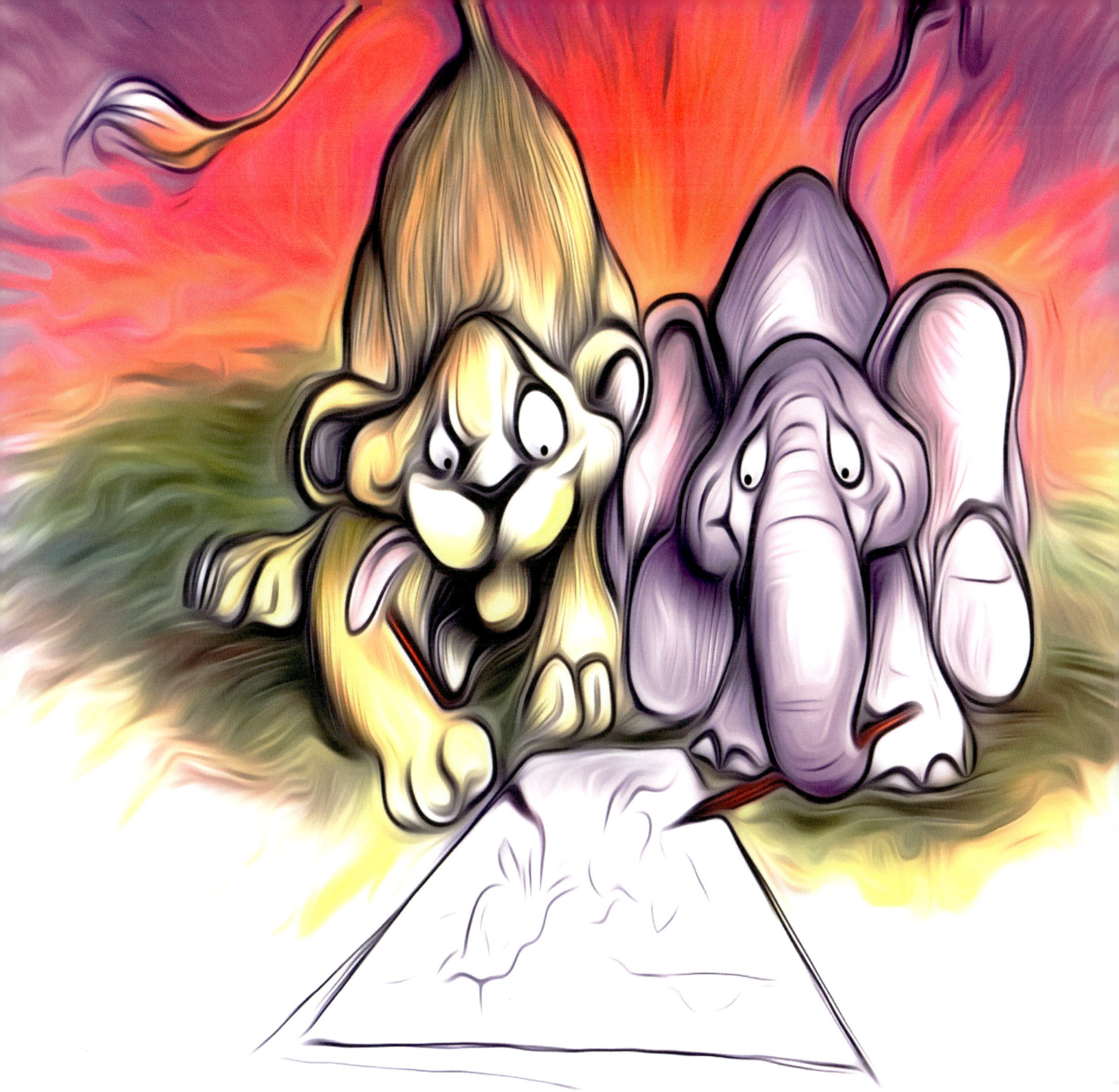

They drew birds and trees,
rivers and lakes,
Then Javiah thanked the elephant
and went on his way.

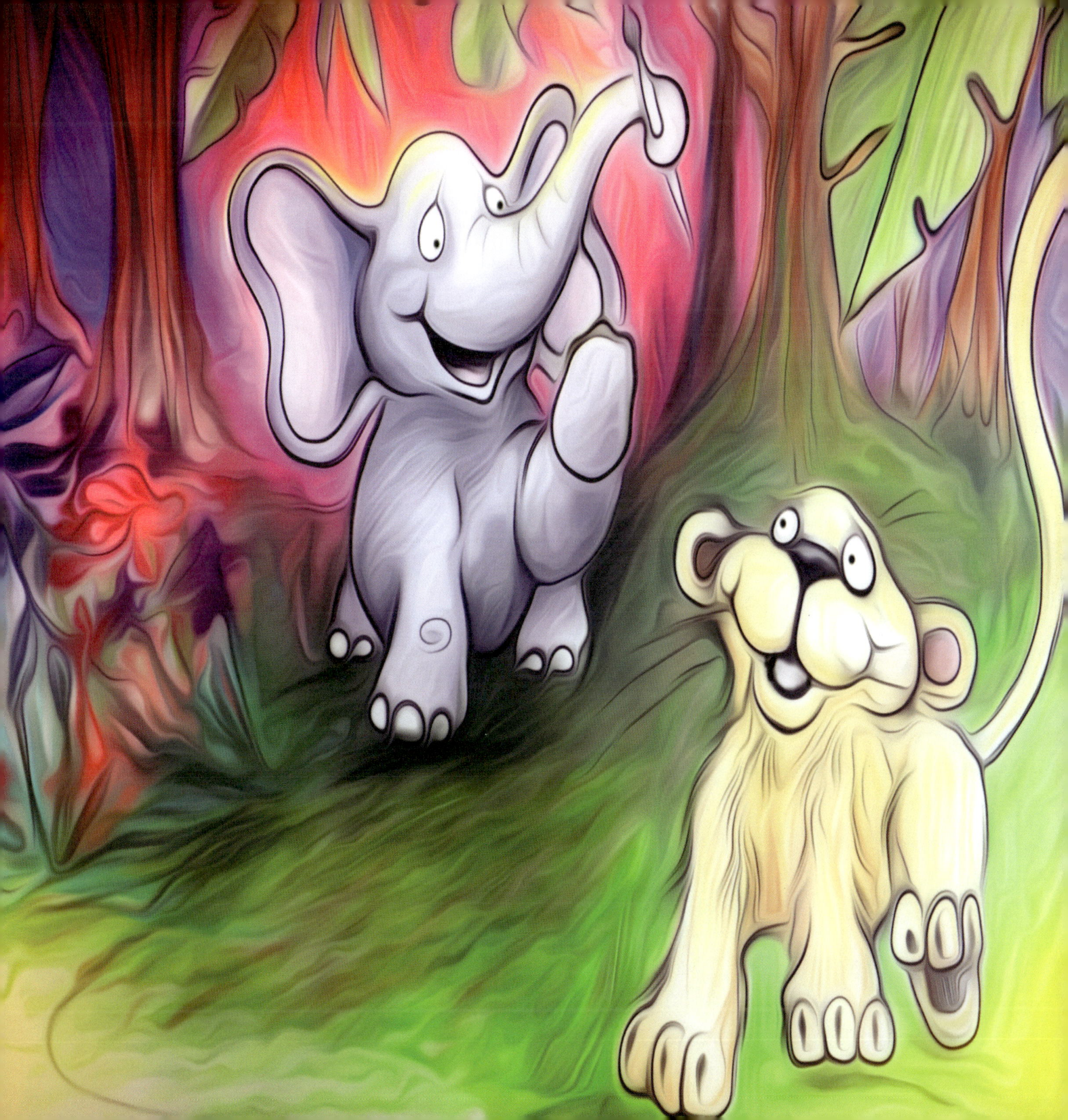

He then saw Amiyah the cheetah,

who sang by the stream,

She sang tunes and rhythms

sweet like a dream.

Animals would listen

whilst grazing by the pond

As the melodies travelled far and beyond.

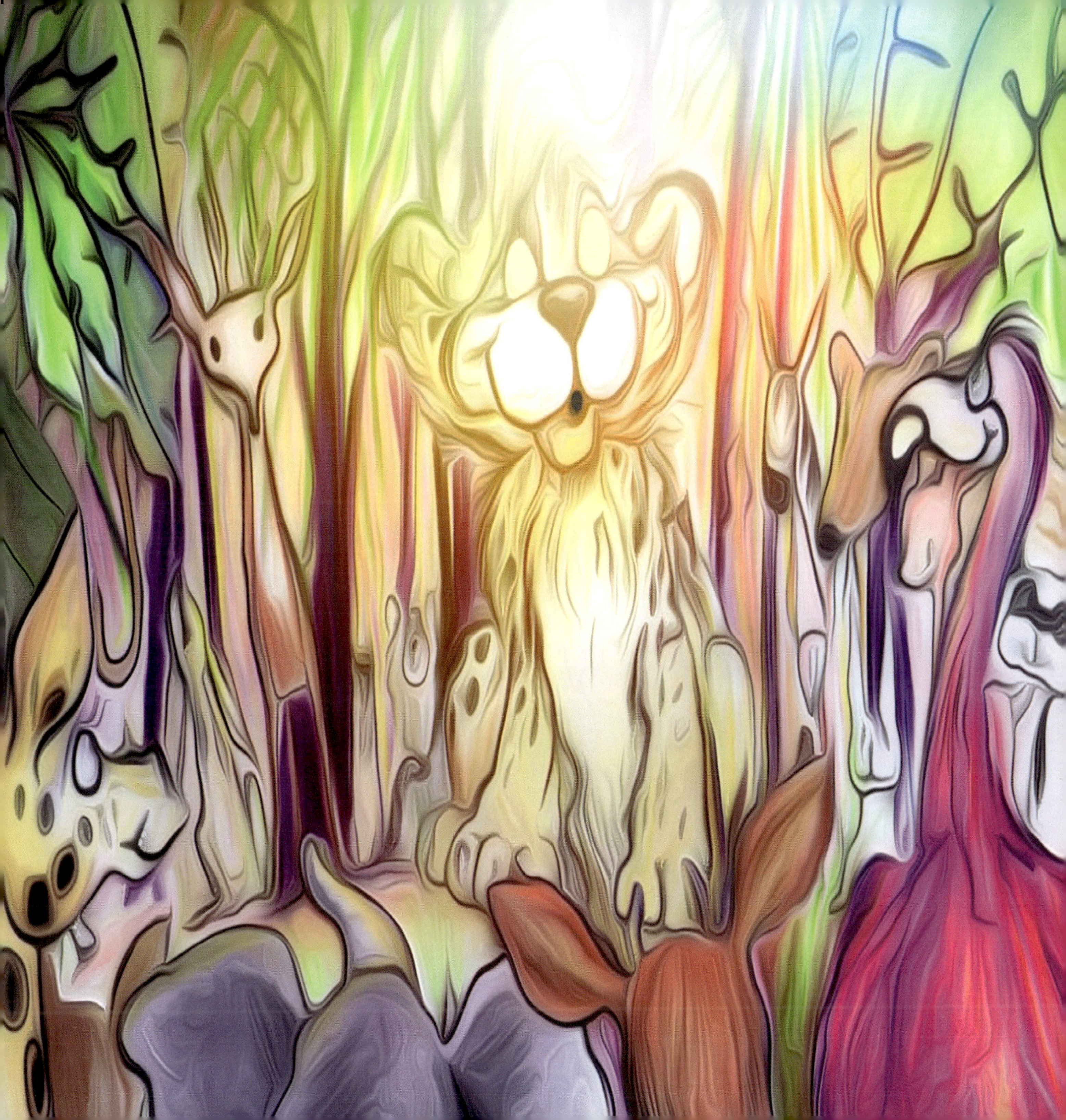

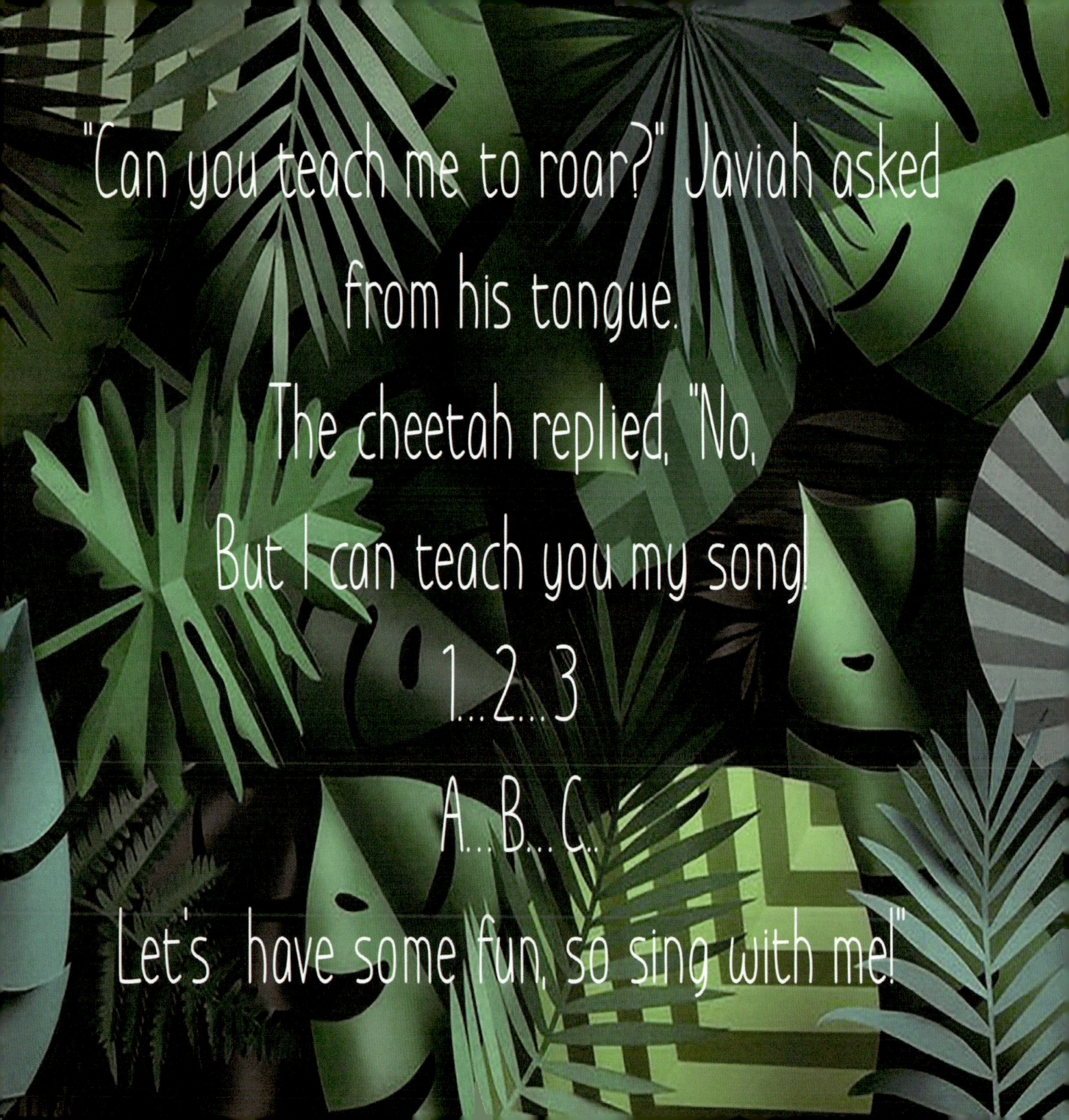

"Can you teach me to roar?" Javiah asked from his tongue.

The cheetah replied, "No, But I can teach you my song!

1...2...3

A...B...C...

Let's have some fun, so sing with me!"

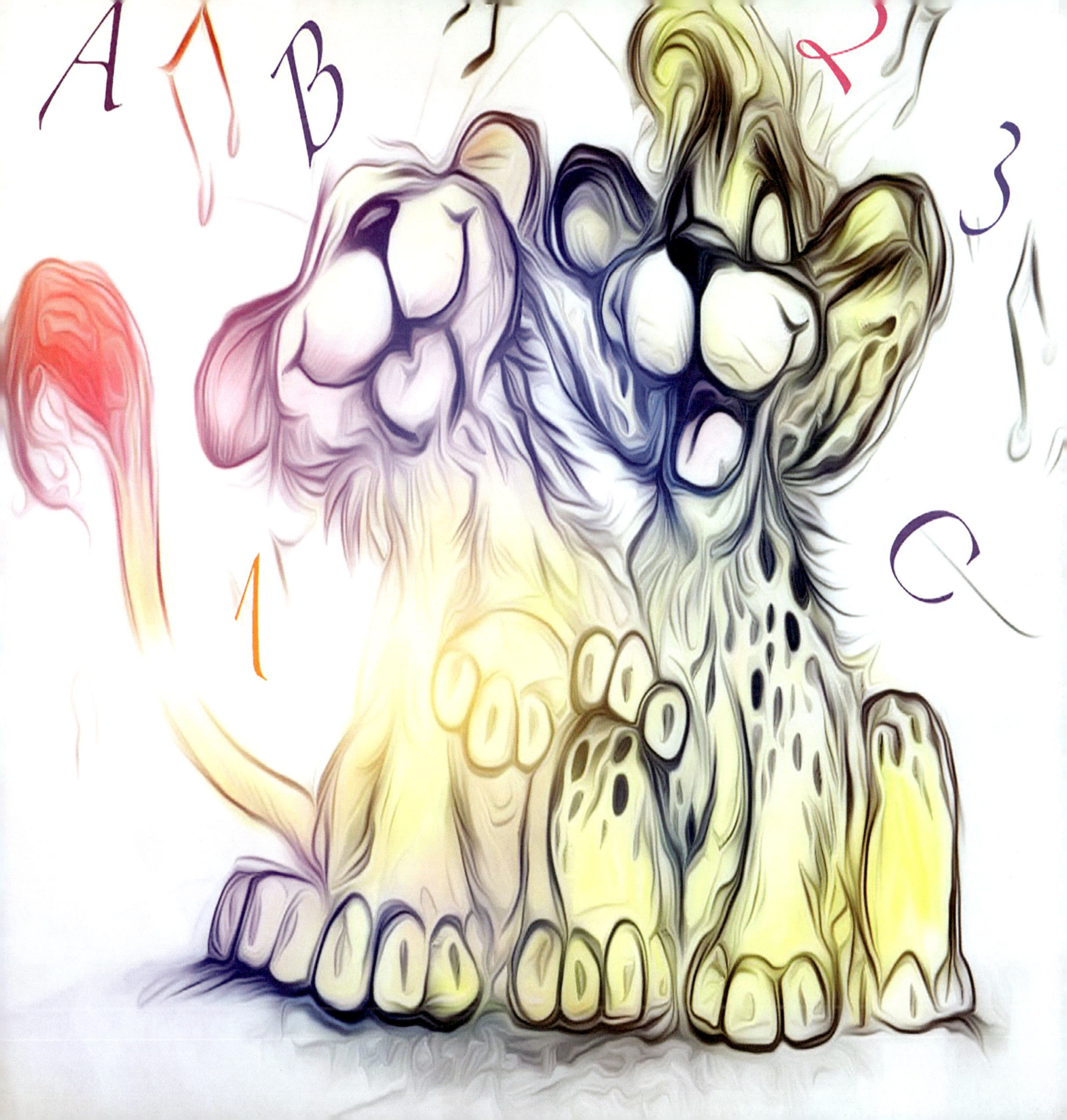
A
B
3
1
C

He sang the song
and his singing was good,
With each number and letter understood.
"That was really fun!" Javiah said,
As he left the cheetah
and went on ahead.

Although he could sing, dance
and even could draw,
Javiah the lion
still could not roar.

Then he saw daddy
who was a determined lion.
He kept on pushing him,
so he kept on trying.

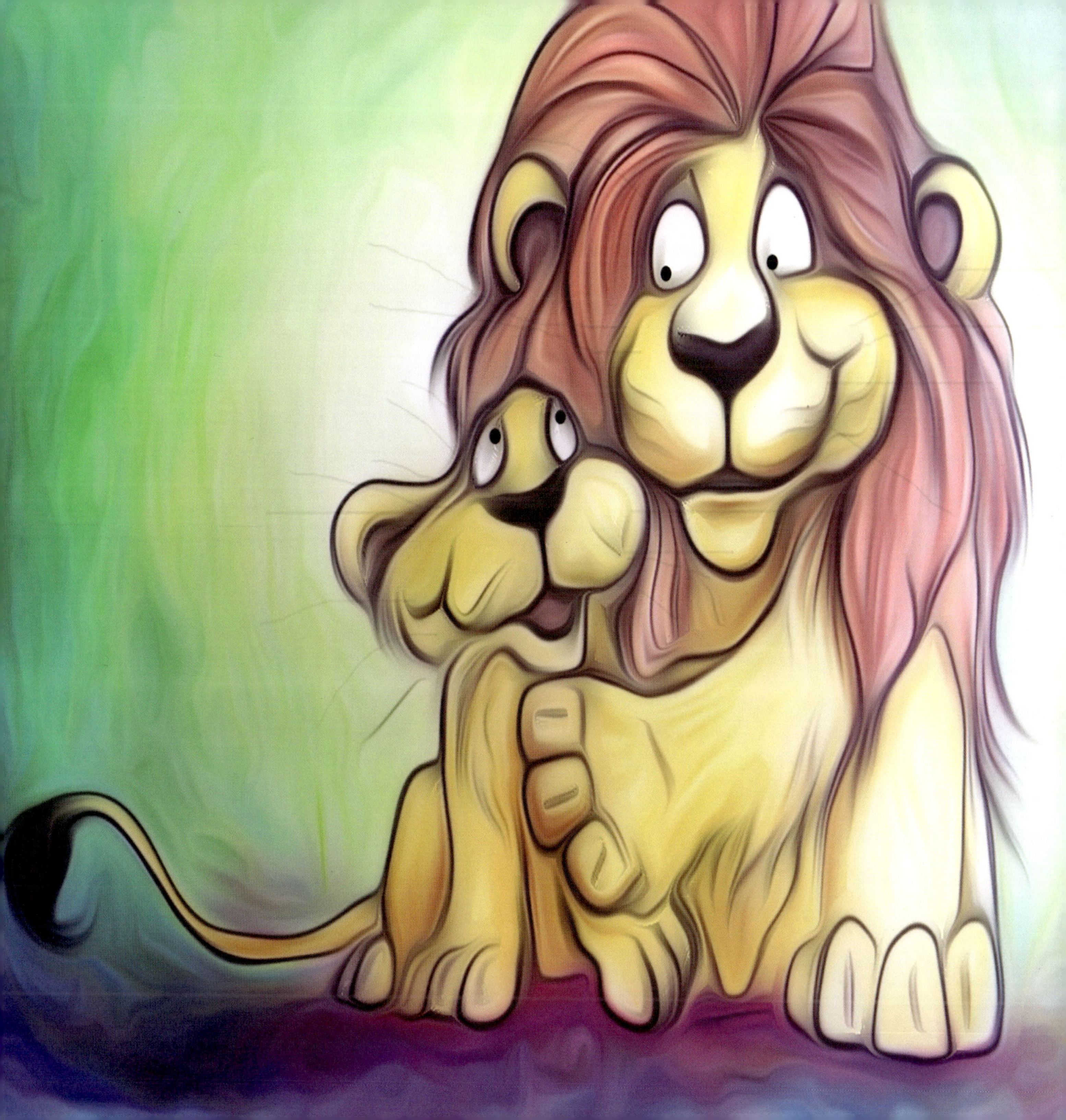

He gave one more go with nothing to fear,

And let out a big huge...

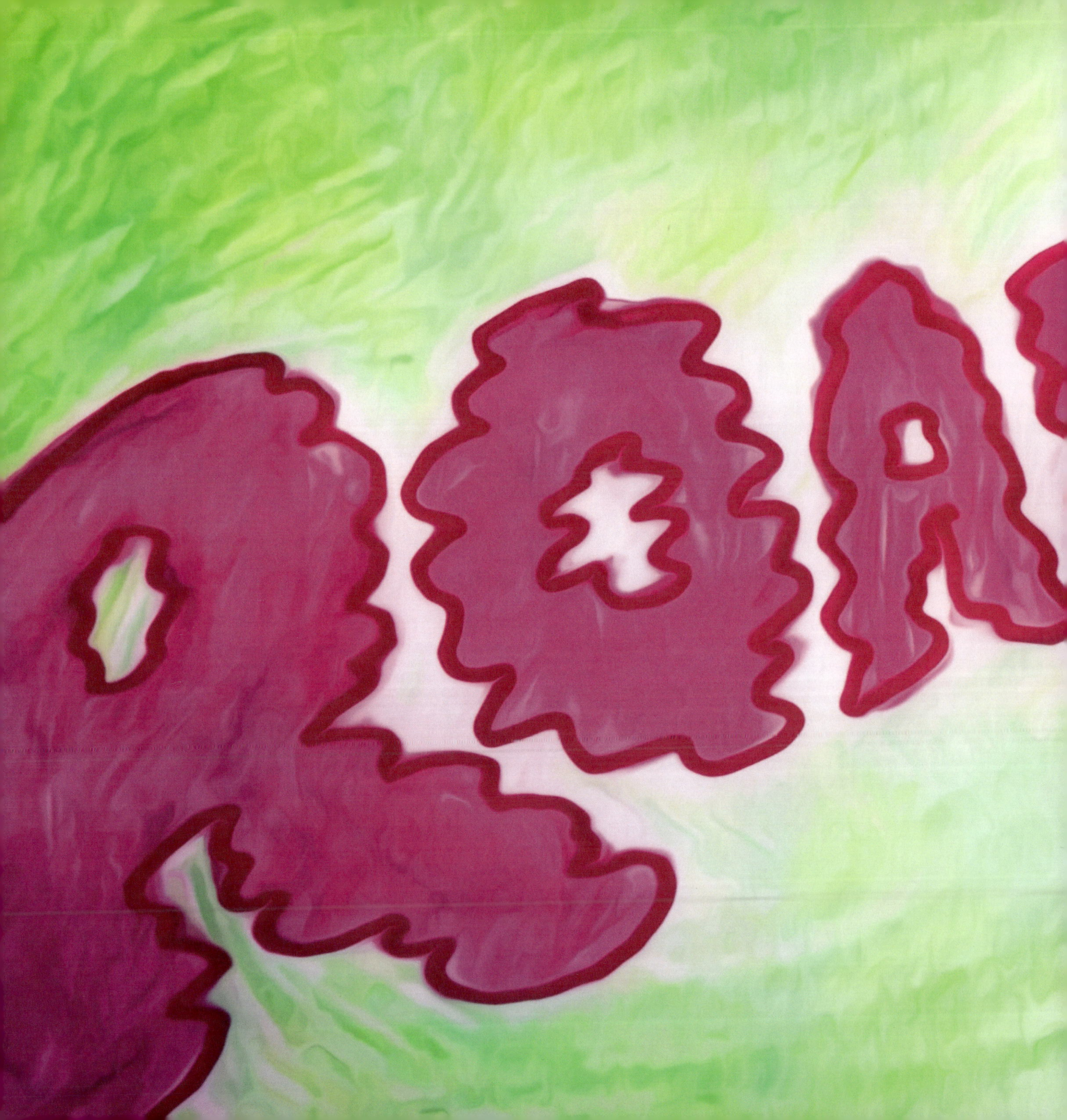

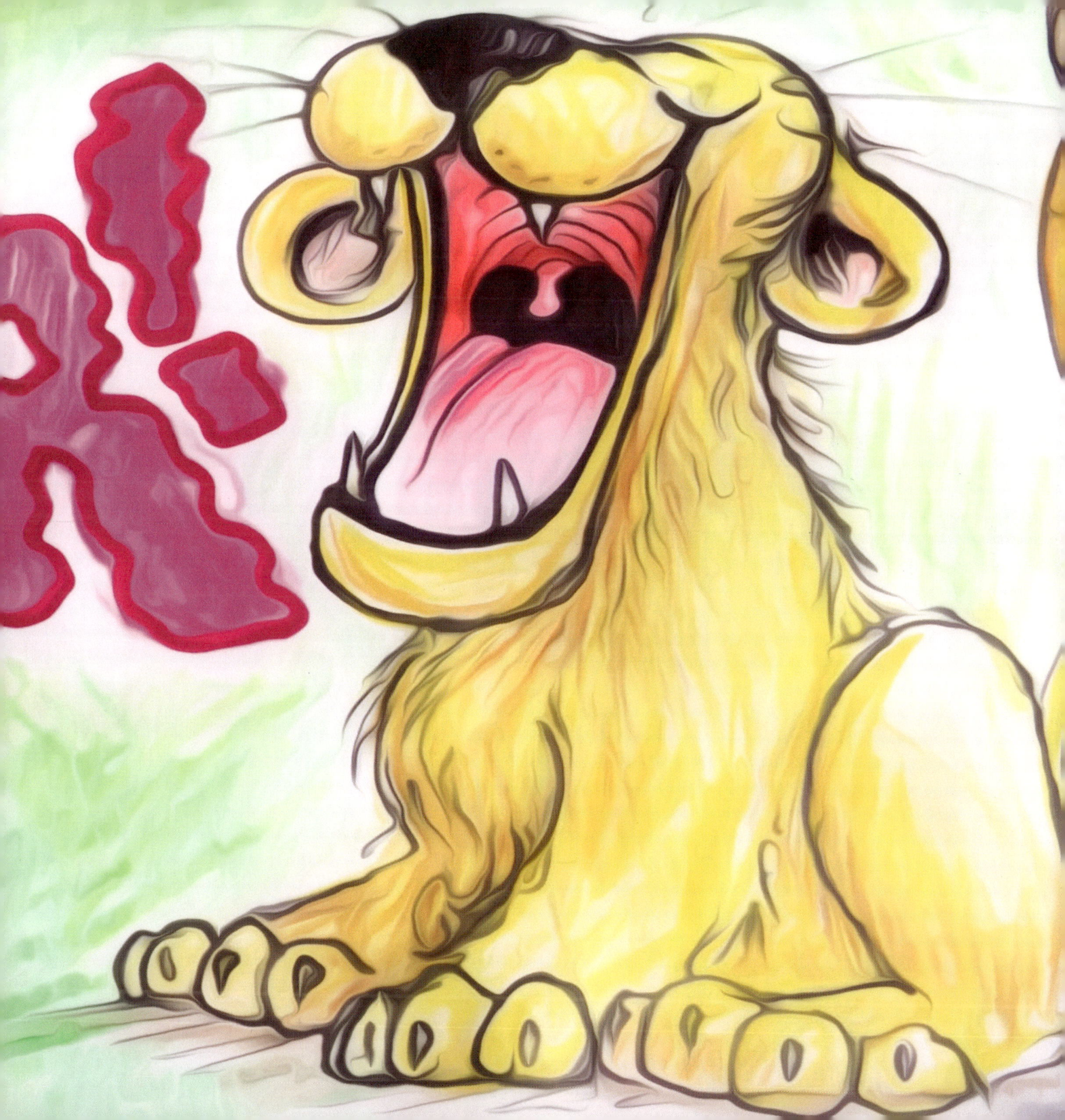

For the whole jungle to hear!

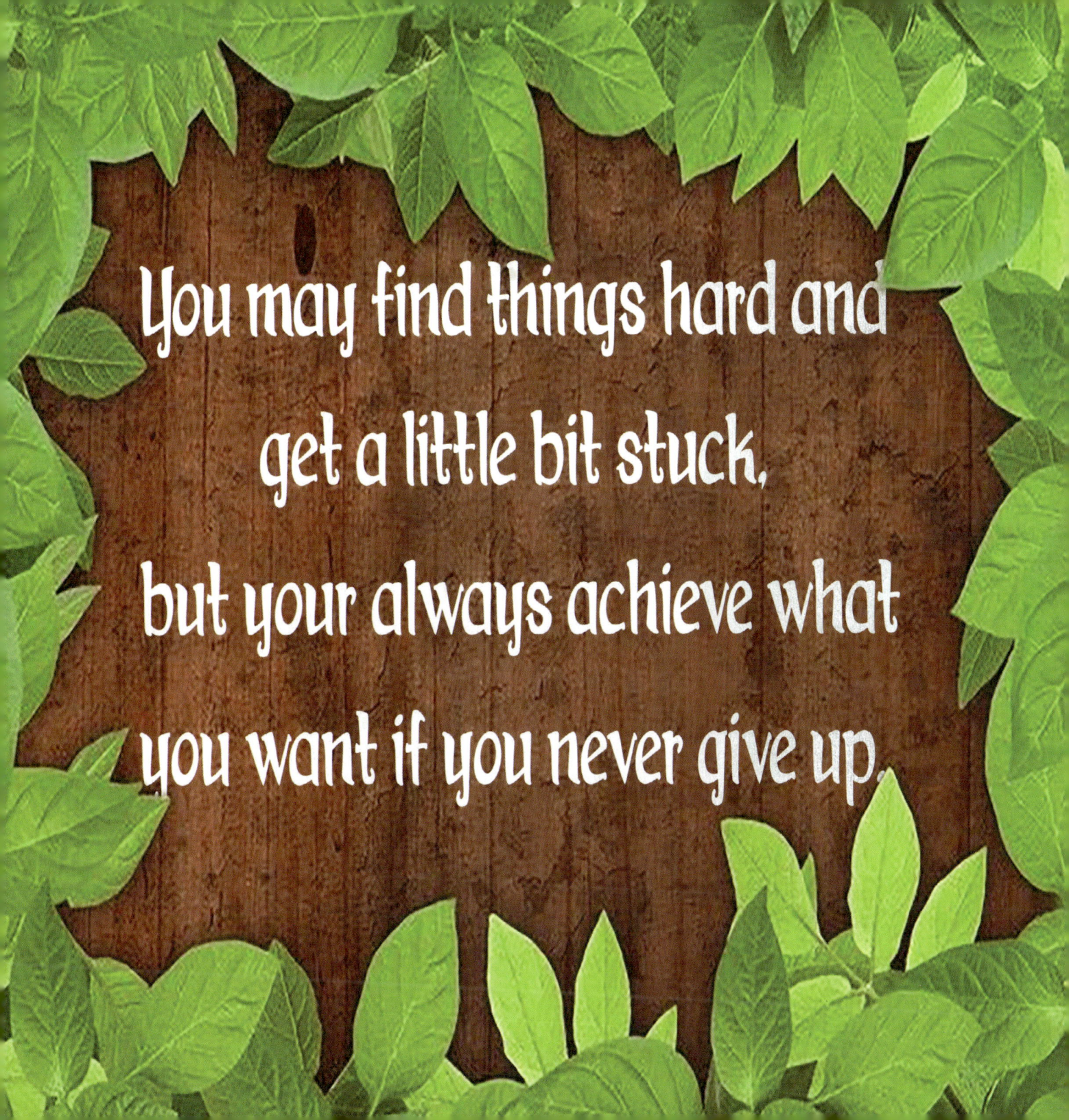

You may find things hard and get a little bit stuck, but your always achieve what you want if you never give up.

The End

Special thanks
to all who helped me along my journey
and to my "Little Lion" who inspired me to write this book.

WIGGAWOOS

Printed in Great Britain
by Amazon